Olivia the Orchid Fairy

For Laura Rouffiac, who loves fairies (and bunnies!)

Special thanks to Narinder Dhami

If you purchased this book without a cover, you should be aware that this book is stolen property. It was reported as "unsold and destroyed" to the publisher, and neither the author nor the publisher has received any payment for this "stripped book."

No part of this work may be reproduced, stored in a retrieval system, or transmitted in any form or by any means, electronic, mechanical, photocopying, recording, or otherwise, without written permission of the publisher. For information regarding permission, write to Rainbow Magic Limited c/o HIT Entertainment, 830 South Greenville Avenue, Allen, TX 75002-3320.

ISBN-10: 0-545-07094-5
ISBN-13: 978-0-545-07094-2

Copyright © 2007 by Rainbow Magic Limited.

All rights reserved. Published by Scholastic Inc., 557 Broadway, New York, NY 10012, by arrangement with Rainbow Magic Limited.

SCHOLASTIC, LITTLE APPLE, and associated logos are trademarks and/or registered trademarks of Scholastic Inc. RAINBOW MAGIC is a trademark of Rainbow Magic Limited. Reg. U.S. Patent & Trademark Office and other countries.

12 11 10 9 8 7 6 5 4 3 2 1   9 10 11 12 13/0

Printed in the U.S.A.

First Scholastic Printing, February 2009

Olivia the Orchid Fairy

by Daisy Meadows

SCHOLASTIC INC.
New York   Toronto   London   Auckland   Sydney
Mexico City   New Delhi   Hong Kong   Buenos Aires

The Fairyland Palace

Blossom Hall

Fairy Garden

Leafley Village

Visitors' Center

Jack Frost's Ice Castle

Blossom Lake

Picnic Spot

The Park

Petal Perfection Flower Shop

Blossom Village High St

Rainbow Falls Gardens

Chaney Court Flower Show

I need the magic petals' powers,
To give my castle garden flowers.
I plan to use my magic well
To work against the fairies' spell.

From my wand ice magic flies,
Frosty bolts through fairy skies.
This is the crafty spell I weave
To bring the petals back to me.

Contents

Out and About   1

Goblins in the Garden   13

Rainbows, Rainbows, Everywhere!   21

Ice Falls   31

Flower Trail   45

Purple Perfection   57

Out and About

"Welcome to Rainbow Falls Gardens," said the man behind the desk. He picked up a garden map and counted out six tickets. Then he passed them all over the counter. "I hope you enjoy your day!"

Kirsty Tate smiled at her friend Rachel Walker as their parents thanked the man and picked up the tickets. The two families headed through the wrought-iron gates that stood at the entrance to the gardens. The Tates and the Walkers were spending spring vacation together, and so far they were having a magical time! Kirsty and Rachel hoped today would be just as exciting.

As they walked through the gates, the girls found themselves at the edge of a large grassy lawn, with a cluster of trees at the far end. The sun was warm on their faces, and they could hear birds singing.

"Let's see," Mr. Walker said, opening up the map. "Where should we go first?"

Rachel, Kirsty, and Mr. Walker looked at the map. There was an orchid garden, an arboretum, and of course, the famous Rainbow Falls.

"I want to see the waterfall first," Rachel said eagerly.

"Ah," said Mr. Walker. "I was just about to suggest the arboretum."

"What's an arboretum?" Kirsty asked.

"It's an area with lots of beautiful trees and shrubs," her dad told her, coming over to look at the map, too.

"*Woof!*" barked Buttons, the Walkers' dog, pulling hard on his leash.

"I think Buttons wants to see the arboretum, too." Mrs. Walker laughed.

"I think I'd like to see the falls," Kirsty said. "Can we go there and meet you at the arboretum afterward?" she asked her parents.

"I don't see why not," Mr. Tate agreed.

"We'll see you at the entrance to the arboretum in an hour," Mrs. Tate told the girls. Then she frowned slightly as she glanced at the nearby flowerbeds. "I hope the trees in the arboretum are healthier than these flowers," she said.

"Look, half of them are drooping or dead!"

Rachel and Kirsty exchanged glances. They knew exactly why the flowers didn't look as beautiful as they should. Unknown to their parents, the girls were secret friends with the fairies and often helped them when they were in trouble. This time, Rachel and Kirsty were helping the Petal Fairies find their missing magic petals. The petals made flowers bloom and grow beautifully in Fairyland and in the human world. So while the petals were missing, flowers all over the world were wilting and dying!

"I hope we find one of the petals today," Kirsty whispered to Rachel.

"These flowers really need some fairy magic!"

"Definitely," Rachel agreed.

The fairies had shown the girls how Jack Frost had sent his goblins to steal all seven magic petals from Fairyland. He wanted the petals so he could make flowers grow in the freezing gardens around his Ice Castle. But when Jack Frost's icy magic had collided with the Petal Fairies' own spell to get their petals back, the seven petals were caught up in a huge magical explosion. It had sent the petals whirling into the human world.

Kirsty and Rachel had already helped the Petal Fairies find the tulip petal, the poppy petal, the lily petal, and the sunflower petal, but there were still three petals left to find. And the girls knew that Jack Frost's goblins were looking for them, too.

"Okay then, we'll see you later, girls," Rachel's mom said with a smile. "Have fun!"

The four adults set off toward the arboretum, with Buttons racing excitedly ahead of them. Meanwhile, Rachel and Kirsty headed down a different path toward Rainbow Falls.

Just as they were walking past a trail that led to the orchid garden, Kirsty heard a nasty chuckle.

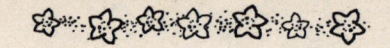

"Did you hear that?" she whispered to Rachel. "It sounded like a goblin."

Rachel nodded. "Let's take a look in the orchid garden," she whispered.

The girls crept down the path to the orchid garden, looking carefully all around them. Goblins always meant trouble! And this time, Jack Frost had armed them with a wand of his own icy magic, which meant they were much more powerful than usual.

It was quiet in the small orchid garden, and the girls couldn't see anyone else in there. It seemed there were only gorgeous, colorful orchids blossoming everywhere. Blooms of yellow, purple, pink, and orange filled every nook and cranny of the flowerbeds. Some orchids were even growing from tree stumps and logs!

"Wow," Kirsty breathed. "They're beautiful!"

Rachel was looking thoughtful. "Almost too beautiful," she pointed out in a low voice. "The orchid petal has been stolen, so they should all be wilting."

Kirsty nodded. "The orchid petal must be nearby," she agreed. "It's the only thing that could be making these orchids so bright and healthy."

The girls knew that each of the seven magical petals helped a particular group of flowers to grow well. The magical orchid petal made orchids bloom all over the world, but it also made sure that purple and blue flowers were healthy and colorful, too.

Kirsty's eyes widened as she spotted a sudden movement in the flowers. Something was rummaging through the orchids! She nervously elbowed Rachel as she spotted a familiar flash of green.

"There's a goblin!" she hissed.

Goblins in the Garden

"Look, another one!" Rachel whispered, pointing to a second goblin on the other side of the garden. "And there are two more!"

"They must be searching for the orchid petal," Kirsty said.

"Well then, we'll have to look for it, too," Rachel declared. "We have to find it before they do!" The two girls crouched down and began peeking into the flowerbeds, hoping to find the magic orchid petal before the goblins noticed them. They hadn't been looking for very long, though, when they heard a triumphant goblin cry, "I've got it! I've got it!"

Rachel and Kirsty looked up and saw a goblin not far from them leaping up and down excitedly. He was waving a purple-and-blue petal in one hand.

"The orchid petal!" Kirsty groaned as he raced off toward his friends.

The girls jumped to their feet as the goblin ran across the garden. A large raised flowerbed was in his path. He tried to jump over it, but he tripped and fell into a patch of mud instead.

Rachel grabbed Kirsty's hand. "Come on," she called. "Let's try to get that petal!"

The girls hurried to the goblin and stood over him.

"The fairies will be really angry with you if you don't give that back," Kirsty warned. "And you should know, Olivia the Orchid Fairy is probably on her way here right now!"

The goblin sat up and brushed the mud off himself. Then he rudely stuck out his tongue. "I don't care!" he insisted, clutching the petal.

Just then, the air seemed to shimmer around them, and a tiny fairy darted into view.

Rachel smiled. "Olivia!" she cried.

Olivia the Orchid Fairy fluttered in midair. She had glossy dark hair that was pulled back in a ponytail, and she wore a purple dress with bell sleeves and a wide yellow belt. "Hello, girls," she sang. "I see you've found my petal."

The goblin with the petal stood up and backed away. "Uh-oh," he murmured nervously. Then he spotted his friends across the garden. "Hey!" he shouted to them. "Help!"

Six other goblins rushed over. Kirsty noticed that one of them, a goblin with extremely large feet, was carrying the magic wand.

"The orchid petal is mine," Olivia told the goblins. "And I'd like it back, please."

"Come any closer, fairy, and I'll turn you into an ice cube," the goblin with the wand threatened. "Run!" he ordered his friends. They took off across the garden as fast as they could go.

Then the goblin with the wand grinned and made a mean face. "You'll never see that petal again," he told the girls. "Never!" And with that, he let out a nasty laugh and raced out of the garden at top speed.

Rainbows, Rainbows, Everywhere!

"Quick! After them!" Kirsty shouted, running along the path with Rachel close behind.

Olivia zoomed through the air next to them. "It'll be faster if we all fly," she said, pointing her wand at the girls. A sparkling stream of purple-and-blue fairy dust swirled around Kirsty and Rachel, instantly turning them into fairies.

"Thanks, Olivia," Rachel said, flapping her glittery wings in delight. "Now let's catch up with those goblins."

The three friends flew through the air, following the pesky green figures. They were beginning to gain on the goblins when they rounded the corner. Rachel and Kirsty gasped at the sight — Rainbow Falls was straight ahead of them. Water plunged from high rocks into a large, deep pool just in front of the goblins. The fine spray from the waterfall was making rainbows shimmer and dance in the air above the wet rocks in the pool. The girls hovered in midair, gazing with wonder at the sight.

There were signs all around the falls saying that no one should climb on the slippery rocks. The goblins ignored all the signs. One by one, they started leaping onto the nearest rock.

"They're not going in the pool, are they?" Kirsty said in surprise. "Goblins hate getting their feet wet!"

"They're using the rocks as stepping stones," Rachel realized. "They're going to get away with that petal!"

Olivia sighed. "Come on, let's follow them," she said, and the three girls fluttered after the goblins. "You know, all these little rainbows remind me of the ones we've used to travel to Fairyland," Kirsty said. Then she smiled as an idea struck her. "You know, I just thought of something that might stop the goblins!" she said to her friends in a low voice. "Just go along with what I say, OK?"

Rachel and Olivia nodded, looking curious.

Kirsty winked at them and then said loudly, "Isn't it lucky that the goblins came to Rainbow Falls? Do you think they noticed that these little rainbows are just like the magical rainbow bridges the fairy king and queen use to bring people to the Fairyland Palace?"

Rachel tried to hide a smile as she realized what her friend was up to. Kirsty was trying to trick the goblins! Olivia seemed to have caught on, too, because she was agreeing loudly. "Yes, they're exactly like the rainbow bridges," she said. "And a rainbow bridge will whisk you straight to the fairy king and queen if you step into one. It's powerful magic!"

Rachel nudged Kirsty with glee. It was obvious that the goblins had heard what the girls had been saying. They now looked extremely nervous, all huddled together on a stepping stone. They were muttering anxiously about being whisked off to answer to the king and queen of Fairyland.

A rainbow formed right over the head of one goblin, and he pulled away from it. "No! I don't want to go to Fairyland!" he exclaimed.

A second rainbow appeared near the goblin with the orchid petal. "Me neither. No way!" he yelped, hopping to a different stone.

Then the goblin holding the wand let out a squeal as a rainbow appeared right in front of his face. "Ooh! I don't like this!" he wailed.

Kirsty and Rachel looked at one another. "They're so nervous, they're not thinking about the petal at all now," Kirsty whispered.

Rachel nodded. "This might be a good chance for us to try and grab it," she suggested.

"Good thinking," Olivia agreed. "If we all swoop down together, hopefully we'll catch them by surprise and we can get my petal back."

"Let's try," Kirsty said, looking determined. "One, two, three . . . GO!"

Ice Falls

The three fairies zoomed toward the goblins. Unfortunately, the goblins saw them coming.

"Oh no you don't!" one shouted, splashing water at the girls.

Kirsty dodged the spray, but Rachel wasn't so quick, and her wings became heavy with water. She shook them out and backed away, trying to flap them dry.

Laughing, the goblins flicked more water at the fairies, until all three of them were forced to back off.

"That's right, fly away," the goblin with the wand sneered. He put his hands on his hips, but then jumped as another rainbow appeared right by one of his elbows. "Stupid rainbows! They're really getting on my nerves!" he snapped.

But the goblin with the petal was looking thoughtful. "How do we know these rainbows are magic, anyway?" he said. "What if those fairies are trying to trick us, like they did with the sunflower petal yesterday?"

Kirsty and Rachel exchanged a worried glance. Would the goblins realize that the rainbows were actually completely harmless?

"If you think it's all a trick, why don't

you step into one of them and find out?" a skinny goblin challenged.

"Why should I do it?" the goblin with the petal replied. "You try it!" And he gave the skinny goblin a shove toward the nearest rainbow.

"Yikes!" yelled the skinny goblin, falling straight through the rainbow and into the pool with a splash. "Hey! It's freezing in here!" he shouted, struggling to climb out. The other goblins ignored his complaints. They were far too excited after learning that the girls had tricked them.

"Those rainbows aren't magic at all!" one of them yelled, looking victorious.

The goblin with the wand pulled the skinny goblin out of the water, and then glared up at the fairies. "It's time to teach those tricky fairies a lesson, once and for all," he declared. "This spell will freeze you into ice. No more fairies, won't that be nice?" he shouted, pointing the wand at them.

"Quick!" yelled Rachel. "Fly away!"

Three icy bolts of magic poured from the wand toward the girls and Olivia. Hearts pounding, Kirsty and Rachel zoomed away from the freezing magic, with Olivia whizzing alongside.

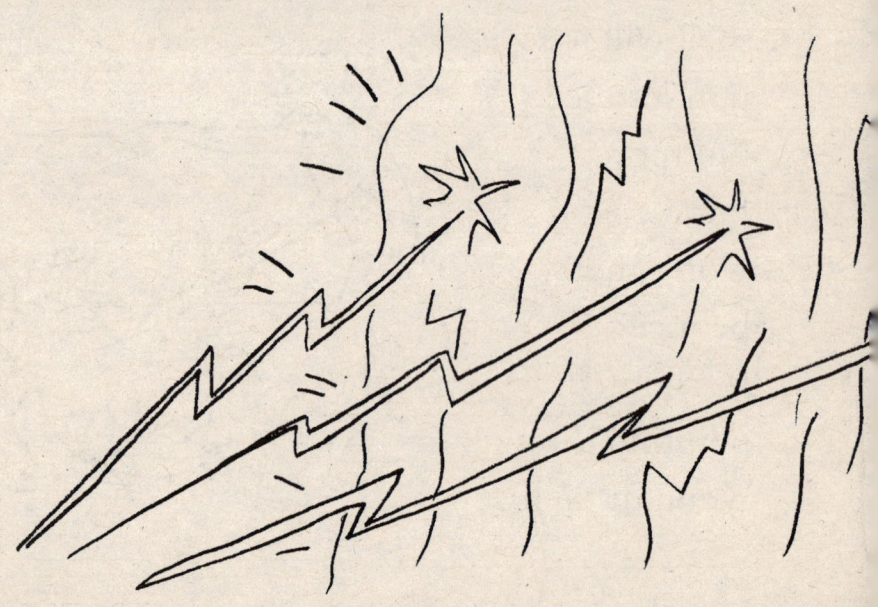

The ice bolts just barely missed the three friends and struck Rainbow Falls instead. Kirsty, Rachel, and Olivia stopped and stared in amazement as the entire waterfall and the pool below turned to solid ice, and the roar of the water was silenced immediately.

"Wow!" Kirsty gulped. "It's beautiful!"

Even the goblins seemed amazed by the icy waterfall. The magic had frozen every drop of water in an instant.

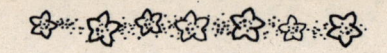

Even the splashes of spray were frozen in midair, like twinkling diamonds.

A shout from one of the goblins broke the silence. "Hey, we can walk across the pool now!"

Rachel looked down to see that the goblins were skidding and sliding across the ice. "They're heading around the back of the waterfall," she said. "Let's follow them."

The three fairies flew after the goblins, who had now crept into the icy cave behind the frozen waterfall. Kirsty, Rachel, and Olivia swooped into the cave after them, swerving to avoid the gleaming icicles that now hung from its roof.

"Where are they? Which way did they go?" Rachel asked. Looking around the ice cave, she saw no sign of the goblins.

The water had frozen into unusual twisted shapes, a lot like crystal sculptures. The sun shone through them, making them glitter and sparkle with a bright, white light. "It's so beautiful," Kirsty said, wide-eyed. "Like a magical ice world."

Rachel nodded. "It's like a frozen Fairyland," she said in awe, "all glittery and sparkly. But there isn't a goblin in sight."

"We'll have to search for them," Olivia said. "They must be here somewhere." The three friends fluttered around the cave, looking behind every icicle in search of the goblins. "There are so many places the goblins could hide." Kirsty sighed, seeing pathways leading in all directions. "It's like a maze in here!"

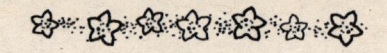

Just then, Rachel let out a cry. "Look, there's a flower!" she called, pointing to the icy wall on her left.

Kirsty and Olivia fluttered over to see a bright purple orchid blooming right out of the ice.

"Only my petal could have done that," Olivia said, looking excited. "Orchids take lots of love and a long time to grow that big!"

Kirsty's face lit up as she saw another orchid, an orange one this time, further down the cave wall. She pointed to it with delight. "It's a trail of flowers!" she cried. "The goblins must have gone this way!"

Flower Trail

The three friends followed the trail of orchids along the passage. Then Olivia swooped in front of Kirsty and Rachel, motioning for them to stop. "I can hear the goblins whispering ahead," she said in a low voice. "We can't let them see us. They might try to turn us into ice again!"

Rachel and Kirsty nodded. They certainly didn't like the idea of being frozen solid, like the waterfall.

The three fairies flew a little farther. Olivia led the way, until they came to the edge of a room that was covered in ice. Very carefully, Rachel peeked around the block of ice that stood at the entrance. She could see a row of icicles dangling from the ceiling, and the goblins all huddled together in the small space.

"I'm f–f–f–freezing," one of them moaned, his teeth chattering.

"It's colder than Jack Frost's Ice Castle in here," another agreed, wrapping his arms around himself.

The goblin with the orchid petal was the only one who didn't seem to be bothered by the cold. He was amusing himself by dragging the magic petal along the icy walls, making bright new orchids bloom everywhere.

Drip! A drop of water fell from an icicle onto a goblin's head. "Hey! Who's dripping water on me?" he whined. "Be quiet! Those fairies will hear you!" another scolded him. "Nobody's dripping water on you," a third told him angrily. "Don't be silly!"

"Olivia, could you turn us back into girls now?" Kirsty asked in a whisper, as the goblins continued to bicker. "I think we'll have a better chance of getting the orchid petal that way."

"Of course," Olivia said, waving her

wand over the girls. A stream of purple-and-blue fairy dust poured from the tip of the wand, and then floated around Kirsty and Rachel.

Rachel shivered as she became a girl once more. It felt even colder now that she was standing still, rather than zipping around on her fairy wings. Her teeth began to chatter. Luckily, before the goblins heard the sound, two more goblins started to yell about being dripped on.

"The magic spell is wearing off," Kirsty realized as she noticed water trickle off the icicles. "The ice is melting!"

Drip! Drip! Drip!

"Whose idea was it to sit here, anyway?" the goblin with the wand complained. He yelped as freezing water ran down his back. "Let's get out of here!"

Rachel and Kirsty stepped in front of the goblins as they got up to leave the room. "You're not going anywhere until you give us that magic petal," Rachel said bravely.

The goblins all shook their heads. "There's no way we're going back to Jack Frost without this petal," the one with the wand said. "We're keeping it, and that's that!"

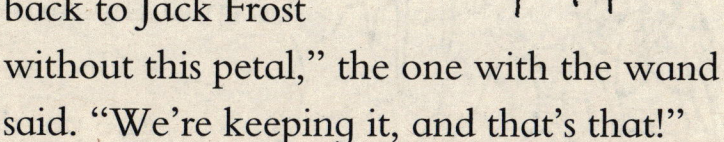

"But haven't you realized that your spell is fading?" Kirsty pointed out. "You can't stay here. Soon, the waterfall will have completely melted!"

"And we are right in the middle of it," Rachel added. "So when the ice melts, we'll all be trapped between these rocks, and the water will be over our heads!" She shuddered at the thought, hoping that the goblins would realize how dangerous the situation was!

Drip! Drip! Drip! Drip!

The goblins looked around nervously as the drops of water started falling faster. "Let us out!" the skinny one cried, trying to push past the girls. "Give us the petal first," Rachel replied, standing firm.

The goblin with the wand pointed it threateningly at the girls, but Olivia let out a tinkling laugh. "Your spell didn't work very well last time, did it?" she reminded him.

"She's right," the skinny goblin muttered, pushing his friend's wand away. "No more magic!"

By now, the drips had turned into little streams, soaking the goblins. "Ugh!" they cried, trying to shield their heads with their arms.

Kirsty and Rachel were getting wet, too.

"We're running out of time," Kirsty said, looking around the cave as water streamed down its walls. "This place is melting fast!"

"You don't really want to end up in the middle of a waterfall, do you?" Rachel asked.

"No!" the goblins wailed miserably. "Let us out!"

Rachel shook her head firmly as melted ice started to pour down like rain. Frustrated and afraid, the goblin with the petal shoved it into Rachel's hands and then barged past her. "We give up, you win!" he moaned, running back the way he'd come.

"Let's get out of here!" shouted another goblin, and all six of the remaining goblins raced after their friend.

Olivia beamed to see her petal safely in Rachel's hands. "Good work, girls!" she cried thankfully, shrinking the petal to its Fairyland size with a wave of her wand.

"The ice is melting quickly now," Kirsty said. "I think we should get out of here."

Rachel nodded, then gasped as a huge chunk of the icy ceiling gave way with a crash. "We only have a few seconds left," she cried. "Run!"

Purple Perfection

"We'll fly out," Olivia called, waving her wand over the girls. "It's quicker."

Kirsty, who'd been slipping and sliding along the slushy ice floor, suddenly felt as light as air, fluttering on sparkly fairy wings again. "Thanks, Olivia. Now let's go!" she shouted gratefully.

The three friends zoomed out of the melting waterfall at top speed. They darted out from beneath the icy cascade in the nick of time. As they turned to look back, there came a great cracking sound and the ice broke from the entrance of the waterfall. At once, water began pouring freely over the falls again, tumbling and crashing into the pool below.

"That was close!" Kirsty whispered, as the roar of the waterfall echoed in the valley. "Thanks, Olivia. I don't think I've ever been so glad to have fairy wings."

Rachel grinned. "Look, there go the goblins," she said. The fairies watched as the goblins grumpily trudged off into the woods.

Olivia gazed at her orchid petal

happily. "Thank you so much, girls. I never would have gotten this back without you," she said. "And now I should take it back to Fairyland where it belongs. Once it's there, I can use its magic to help all the orchids, and the other blue and purple flowers, to grow again."

Kirsty checked her watch. "And it's time for us to meet our parents," she said. "I bet they haven't had half as much fun as we have!"

"I'll send you on your way with a last

bit of fairy magic if you like," Olivia offered. "You'll be girls again when you arrive."

"Oh, thank you," Rachel said eagerly. She loved fairy magic!

Olivia hugged them good-bye and then waved her wand over them. Immediately, the girls were surrounded by a cloud of glittering blue and purple fairy dust. When it cleared a moment later, they found themselves at the entrance to the arboretum, where they were supposed to meet their parents.

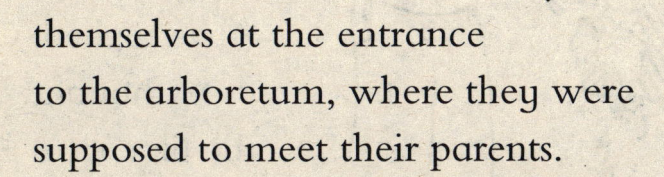

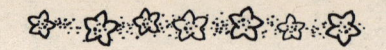

As the last few sparkles vanished at their feet, Kirsty caught sight of her mom and dad strolling along the path to meet them. "Just in time!" she said under her breath to Rachel.

Rachel laughed, then waved at her mom and dad as well. "Hi! How was the arboretum?" she called, bending down to pet Buttons, who had bounded excitedly over to her. Mr. Walker looked disappointed. "Well, it wasn't quite as good as I'd hoped," he replied. "I thought the lilac trees would be flowering by now, but there wasn't a single blossom."

Rachel glanced at Kirsty, guessing it was because the orchid petal had been missing. Hopefully, Olivia would be back in Fairyland with it soon, and then the blue and purple flowers — including the lilacs — would start blooming.

"We found a nice little café where we can go for lunch, though," Mrs. Tate said. "It's just inside the arboretum."

"That sounds great." Kirsty smiled. "I'm starving!"

The two families began walking through the arboretum toward the restaurant. As they did, Rachel and Kirsty spotted some flowering lilac trees and a purple climbing flower that was growing all over an old brick wall.

"Look! The lilacs are blooming here!" Mr. Tate said, surprised.

"And those are beautiful," Mr. Walker said, pointing at the flowers on the wall. "I can't believe we didn't notice them before."

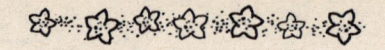

Rachel and Kirsty grinned at each other as they walked along. Olivia's orchid petal was already working its magic with beautiful results!

"Hooray for petal magic!" Rachel said in a whisper.

Kirsty nodded, smiling. "That's five petals we've helped send safely back to Fairyland," she said happily. "I hope we can find the other two before our vacation is over."

Rachel smiled back. She knew they would do their best!

Rainbow Magic
The Petal Fairies

Olivia the orchid fairy has her magic petal back. Now Rachel and Kirsty must help

Danielle
the Daisy Fairy!

Take a look at their next adventure in this special sneak peek!

A Mysterious Message

"Oh!" Rachel Walker panted as she hiked up the steep hill. "I'm really out of breath."

"Me, too," agreed Kirsty Tate, Rachel's best friend. "Even Buttons looks a little tired, and you know how he usually bounces around."

Buttons, the Walkers' shaggy dog, was trotting along next to Rachel, his pink tongue hanging out.

"It'll be worth it when we get to the top, girls," called Rachel's dad. He was walking behind them with Mrs. Walker and Kirsty's parents. "The view will be fantastic. And so will the food," he said, patting a large, straw picnic basket.

A few moments later, Rachel and Kirsty reached the top of the hill. Both girls gasped with delight as they gazed around.

"Blossom Village almost looks Fairyland-size from here!" Rachel whispered to Kirsty.

Kirsty laughed. She and Rachel knew more about fairies than anyone else in the world! The fairies were their special friends, and the girls had visited Fairyland many times.

"This is a lovely spot," said Mrs. Walker. "I hope you all worked up an appetite on that long walk."

Rachel and Kirsty nodded enthusiastically as Mr. Tate opened the picnic basket and began handing out wrapped sandwiches and bags of chips.

As Kirsty was finishing off her chips, she gazed at the little stream bubbling its way down the hill toward a patch of trees. *I wonder where it ends up?* she thought.

Suddenly, to Kirsty's amazement, she saw a beautiful cloud of brilliant silver fairy dust rising from the trees.

Kirsty almost choked on the last bite of her sandwich! As she watched, the silvery sparkles began to drift through the air toward her.

Kirsty knew she and Rachel had to make sure their parents didn't spot the fairy dust. Quickly, she nudged Rachel, who was sitting next to her. Rachel glanced up, and her eyes widened.

"Look, everyone!" Rachel said quickly, pointing in the opposite direction. "There's the big field of sunflowers in Leafley village."

Everyone except Kirsty turned to look where Rachel was pointing. Meanwhile, Kirsty watched excitedly as the silvery sparkles began to form themselves into words. They seemed to be floating right in front of her:

Look around, there's more to see,
A fairy friend says follow me!